VIKING/PUFFIN

Published by the Penguin Group
Penguin Books Ltd, 27 Wrights Lane, London W8 5TZ, England
Penguin Books USA Inc., 375 Hudson Street, New York, New York 10014, USA
Penguin Books Australia Ltd, Ringwood, Victoria, Australia
Penguin Books Canada Ltd, 10 Alcorn Avenue, Toronto, Ontario, Canada M4V 3B2
Penguin Books (NZ) Ltd, 182–190 Wairau Road, Auckland 10, New Zealand

Penguin Books Ltd, Registered Offices: Harmondsworth, Middlesex, England

First published 1997
1 3 5 7 9 10 8 6 4 2

Text copyright © Penguin Books Ltd, 1997
Illustrations copyright © Steve Cox, 1997

The moral right of the illustrator has been asserted

Manufactured in China by Imago

British Library Cataloguing in Publication Data
A CIP catalogue record for this book is available from the British Library

ISBN 0–670–87259–8 Hardback
ISBN 0–140–56209–5 Paperback

BIG MACHINES
ON THE FARM

STEVE COX

Puffin

Viking

SEED DRILL

SOWING SEEDS

11

FRUIT-PICKING TIME

There's a good crop this year.

CURRA
HARVES

Redcurrants make lovely jam.

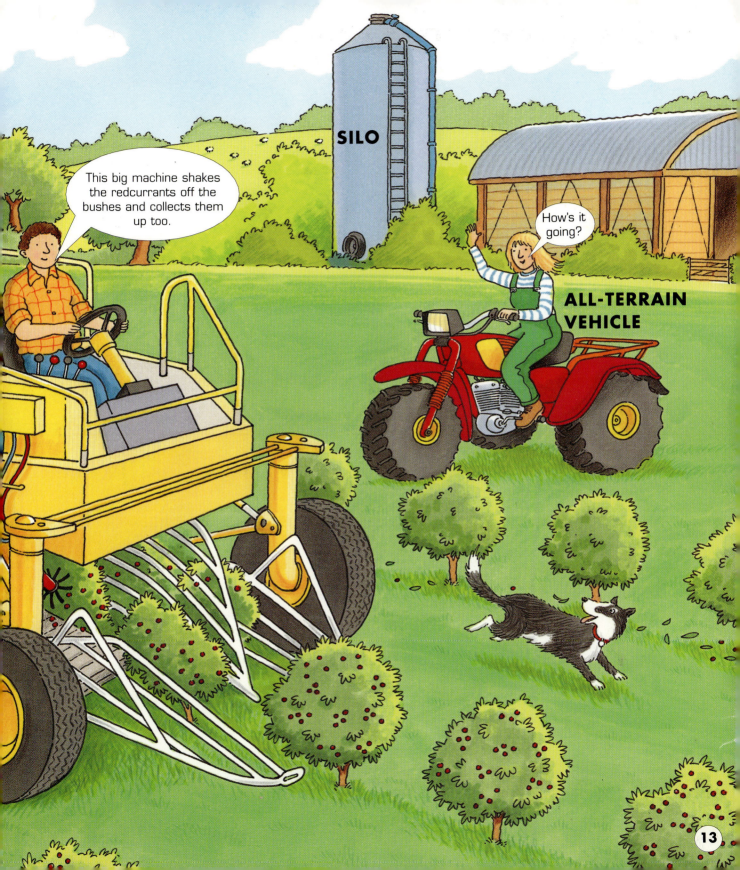

SILO

This big machine shakes the redcurrants off the bushes and collects them up too.

How's it going?

ALL-TERRAIN VEHICLE

ELECTRIC MILKING MACHINE

Yum

That's it, Fred. It can go off to the dairy, now.

AT THE DAIRY FARM

BIG MACHINES ON THE FARM

Follow Farmer Jo and his workers through the pages of this book:

Farmer Jo is ploughing his fields. He drives a tractor which pulls the heavy plough along behind it.

The plough turns over the soil, so that the farmer can plant the seeds. These will grow into next year's crop.

Later Jo checks on his sheep.

"Hello, there!" he calls to Fred, who works on the farm, too.

Fred's tractor is pulling a seed drill. This machine makes holes in the ground and pokes the seeds safely into the earth.

Fred's family help him fill up the drill with seeds.

By spring time some other seeds have grown into potatoes.

Jo's workers use a potato harvester to collect in the crop. The machine digs the potatoes out of the earth and shoots them into a trailer.

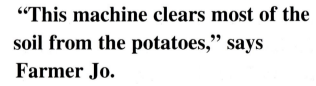

"This machine clears most of the soil from the potatoes," says Farmer Jo.

The summer sun makes the fruit grow.

"Time to pick the juicy redcurrants," says Farmer Jo.

He uses a currant harvester to collect the fruit for him.

He drives the harvester along very slowly. The machine parts the redcurrant bushes in two halves, shakes the currants off inside and collects them in trays. Lots of leaves and twigs fall out of the bottom of the machine.

By the end of the summer the other seeds have grown into wheat. It is harvest time.

The farm workers use a combine harvester to cut the wheat and collect the grain from the top of each stalk. The grain falls into the trailer waiting close by.

Even in winter, Farmer Jo is busy. He has to milk his cows and send the milk to the dairy, where it is put into bottles or cartons for people to drink.

"We love milk!" say the children.

INDEX